Princess Matilda

Written and Illustrated by
Eva Montanari

little bee

I am a very beautiful Princess.

I live in a splendid castle
and I have a stable with three
very fast black horses.

And, of course,
I have many admirers,
who are all hoping one day
to become princes.

I have wonderful parties,
with friends from every corner
of my kingdom.

And I have lots of servants,
who do everything I say.

Or rather,
they're supposed to.

But sometimes they don't.
And instead they give
me orders!

Can you believe that?

I'm a very kind
and generous princess,
but when that happens,
    I get very,
        very angry…

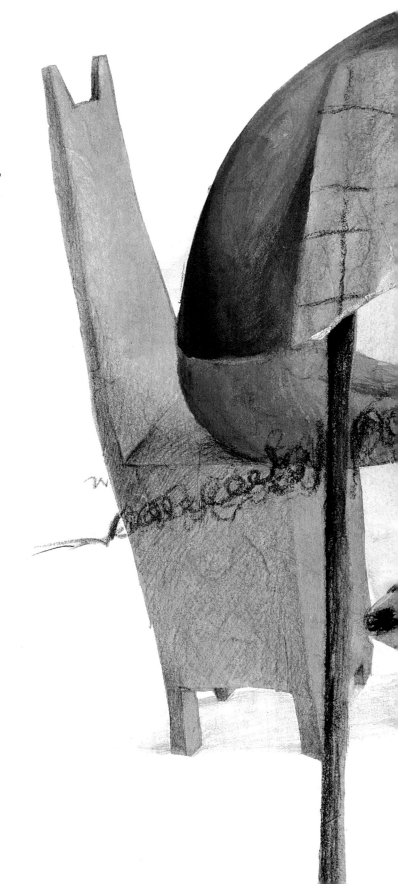

...**angry** like a witch!

I threaten to cook my
servants in a big pot
with all my frogs,
who don't want to be
princes anymore!

But can you believe that?

They're laughing!

It must be because
    I'm a clown with a big red nose!

But even clowns get told off
when they're naughty.

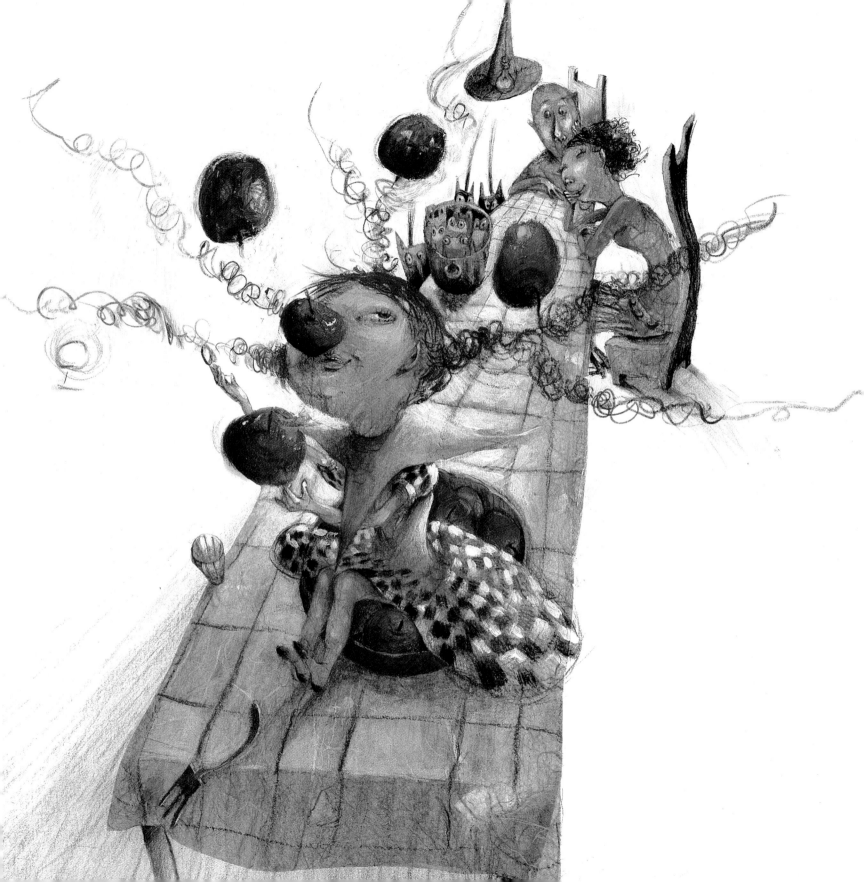

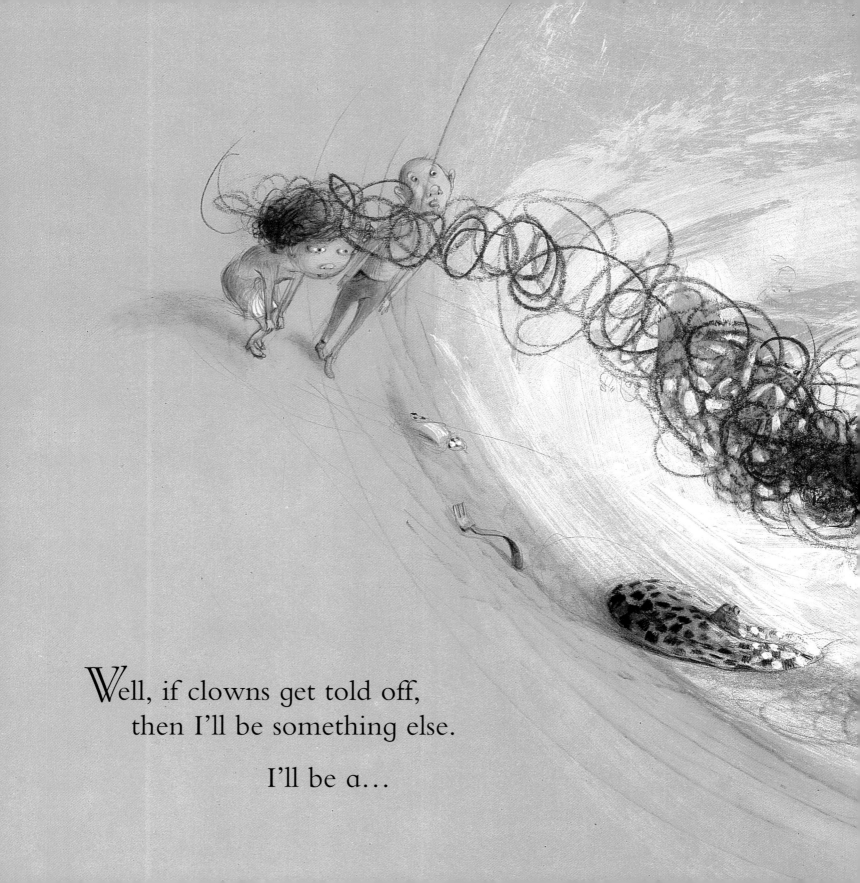

Well, if clowns get told off,
then I'll be something else.

I'll be a...

...butterfly!

Flying free to the end
of the field...

...to a jungle,

where I have somewhere else to live.

There I don't need any servants.
And I don't need my princess's clothes,
or my horses, or my admirers.
I don't need my witch's hat,
or my clown's nose...

...or even my butterfly wings.

Up there I'm
a jungle woman!
I can go wherever I want.

And tonight I'm going to...

...Matilda's room.

She has a bedroom
full of dolls, bears and toys.
And a bed that looks
just like a castle.

In she climbs,
and listens to a story
about a beautiful princess.

A princess who is also called

Matilda.

For my princesses of Strasbourg,
who lived together in a little atelier, drawing other princesses
and sharing nice cake with a little prince inside...

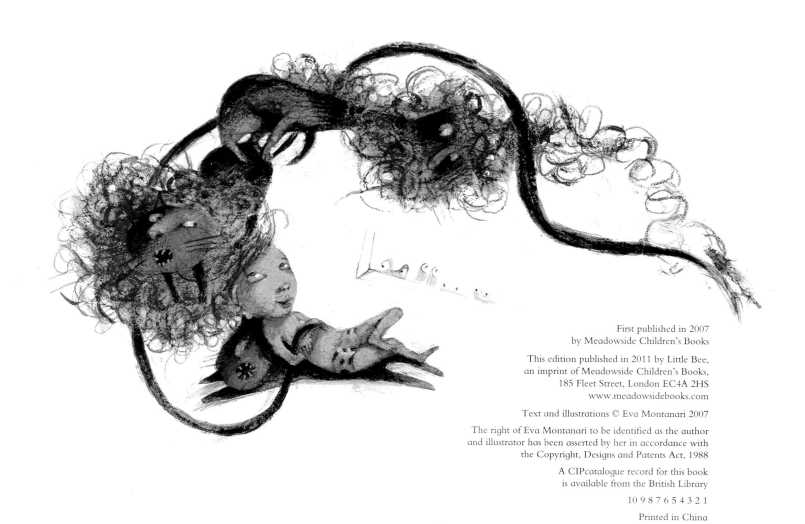

First published in 2007
by Meadowside Children's Books

This edition published in 2011 by Little Bee,
an imprint of Meadowside Children's Books,
185 Fleet Street, London EC4A 2HS
www.meadowsidebooks.com

Text and illustrations © Eva Montanari 2007

The right of Eva Montanari to be identified as the author
and illustrator has been asserted by her in accordance with
the Copyright, Designs and Patents Act, 1988

A CIPcatalogue record for this book
is available from the British Library

10 9 8 7 6 5 4 3 2 1

Printed in China